THIS BLOOMSBURY BOOK

BELONGS TO

....

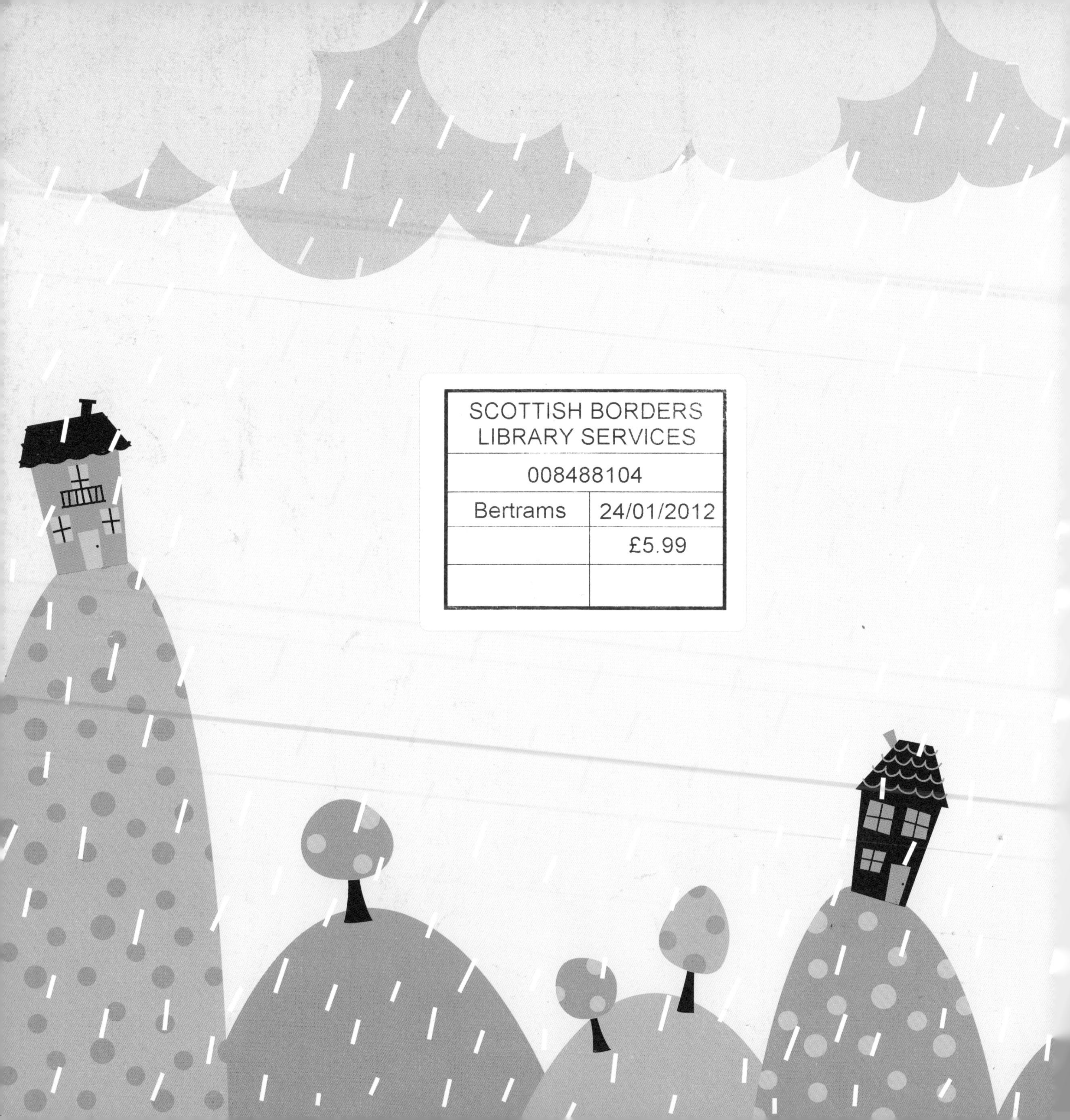

TOO PRINCESSY!

JEAN REIDY

ILLUSTRATED BY

GENEVIÈVE LELOUP

BLOOMSBURY

LONDON BERLIN NEW YORK SYDNEY

TOYS

I AM BORED!

TOO JOLLY, TOO JUMPY
TOYS

TOO DIGGY,
TOO
DUMPY!
TOYS

TOO PIECEY,

TOO BLINKY,
TOYS

TOYS
TOO BANGY,

TOO PLINKY.
TOYS

TOO GOOPY,
TOYS
clay
clay
clay
clay
clay

TOO GLUEY,
Glue
Glue

TOO MARSY,

TOO MOOEY!
TOYS

TOO FUZZY,

TOO SLEEPY,

TOO CRAWLY,
TOO
CREEPY.
TOYS

TOO SOAPY,
TOO SPRINGY,

TOO

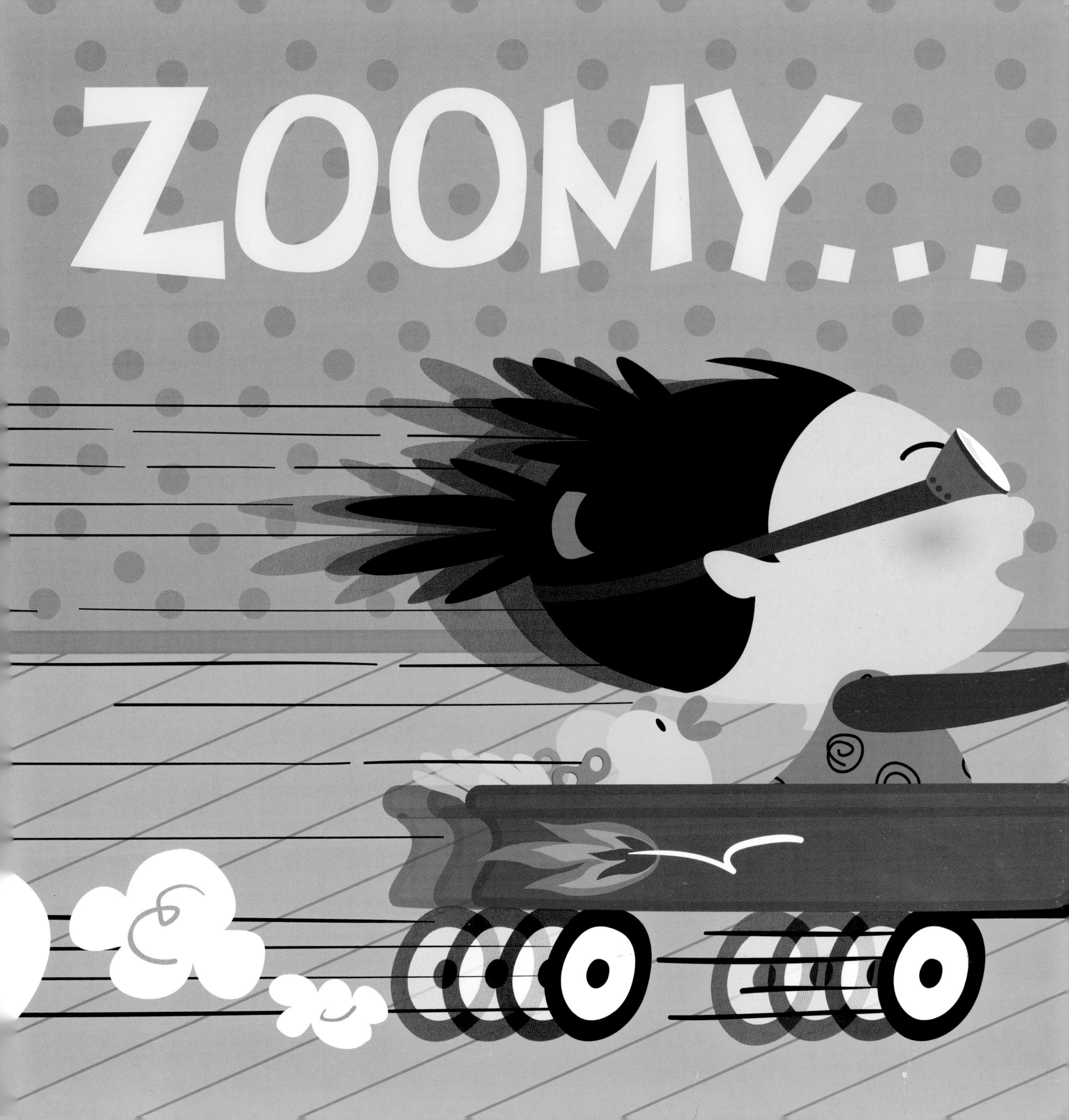
ZOOMY...

TOO RINGY.

TOO CIRCUSY,
TOYS
TOO
CLOWNY,

TOO PRINCESSY!
TOO CROWNY.
TOYS

SO...
TOYS

...FUN! LET'S PLAY.

My favourite things to play on a rainy day:

....

....

....

My favourite things to play on a sunny day:

....

....

....

To Gina and Stephanie –
the original princesses
J.R.

To Charles, who has turned
so many boxes into castles
G.L.

Bloomsbury Publishing, London, Berlin, New York and Sydney

First published in Great Britain in February 2012 by Bloomsbury Publishing Plc
50 Bedford Square, London, WC1B 3DP

A CIP catalogue record for this book is available from the British Library

ISBN 978 1 4088 2694 2

Printed in China by C & C Offset Printing Co Ltd, Shenzhen, Guangdong

1 3 5 7 9 10 8 6 4 2

Book design by Geneviève Leloup

www.bloomsbury.com